City Kids, Country Kids

CHARACTERS
IN ORDER OF APPEARANCE

Narrator

Cassie Barry
a country kid, age 11

Michael Barry
a country kid, age 13

Olivia Sanders
a city kid, age 11

Jada Sanders
a city kid, age 13

Aaron Sanders
a city kid, age 12

SETTING

A big city and a country farm

Narrator: This is a tale about two sets of cousins. Jada, Aaron, and Olivia Sanders lived in the city. Michael and Cassie Barry lived in the country. One day, the country cousins went to visit the city cousins.

Cassie: I can't believe we're actually riding in a taxicab. And look—the buildings are so tall! I'm going to imagine we're in a boat, and the street is a river, and the buildings looming over us are the sides of a canyon. Michael, what do you think of the city so far?

Michael: I think I'm going to throw up from this bumpy cab ride.

Narrator: Meanwhile, in the city cousins' apartment . . .

Olivia: I'm so excited our cousins are coming—I can hardly sit still! It's their first time in the city, and we're going to have so much fun showing them around!

Jada: Just as long as they're not wearing overalls and straw hats.

Narrator: Soon, the two Barry children arrived.

Olivia: Hi, Michael and Cassie! Did you have any trouble finding our apartment?

Cassie: No, we just told the cab driver the address and he knew exactly where to bring us.

Michael: And he was able to find every pothole on the way, too.

Aaron: I guess it must be a big change coming to a place that has millions of people, when you're used to living isolated in the wilderness.

Michael: We don't live isolated in the wilderness! You make it sound like we're pioneers in a covered wagon.

Olivia: But isn't it super boring living way out in the middle of nowhere with nothing to do all day?

Michael: There's plenty to do where we live. We have lots of fun.

Jada: Yeah, right. What's fun about the country? Do you have skate parks or museums or big-league sports arenas?

Cassie: No, but we have a tree house, and there's a movie theater in the next town over.

Jada: Bor-ing! I'm yawning.

Cassie: We have lots of fun in our tree house, Jada. We swing on the ropes, and if a friend comes over, we have a picnic high off the ground.

Jada: Sounds exciting—NOT!

Aaron: Let's take Michael and Cassie with us to the skate park and show them what big-city fun is like!

Jada: I'll bet Cassie and Michael have never even been on skateboards.

Cassie: That's true. There aren't any sidewalks where we live, and many roads aren't paved. You can't really ride a skateboard on a gravel road.

Aaron: Come on and try it—you don't have to be afraid. The helmet and pads will protect you so you won't get hurt—much.

Michael: I'm not afraid! Come on Cassie, let's go. It can't be that hard. All you do is stand on the board and push it with your foot.

Cassie: (*doubtfully*) All right, I'll try.

Narrator: So the five cousins rode the subway to the skate park.

Cassie: The city is so loud and busy, and there's so much traffic zooming by that I'm getting dizzy. I can't believe all these subway trains are zipping around underground. I don't see how you guys know which hole to go down, or which train to get on.

Aaron: We don't think about it. I guess if you live here, you get used to it.

Jada: We also have these new things you've probably never heard of: au-to-mo-biles. We also call them cars.

Olivia: Jada, stop making fun of our cousins and show a little respect!

Narrator: At the skate park, the kids put on their equipment and got ready to skate.

Aaron: Try an ollie, Michael. Put your front foot over the front wheels and your back foot *behind* the back wheels. Then you bend your knees, and . . . pop! See?

Michael: I can do that; it looks easy. Whoops!

Narrator: The next thing Michael knew, he was on his rear end and the skateboard was rolling across the blacktop by itself.

Jada: Ha ha! *Whoom*, and down he goes!

Aaron: Michael, are you all right?

Michael: I'm fine, just get me that skateboard back—because I'm going to do it this time.

Olivia: Remember to push down with your back foot as you're lifting your front foot. See? Pop it!

Michael: Now I see what to do. Thanks. I just need to practice.

Aaron: Do you and Cassie want to try some of the small ramps?

Cassie: Not me. It looks too hard, and kind of scary.

Michael: First, I need to learn how to balance here where it's flat.

Jada: Aw, you two are a couple of scaredy-cats. I guess that's what happens when you live in the country. You're scared of everything except hay and cows. All of you can stay here, but *I'm* heading over to the big half pipe.

Olivia: Cassie, watch Jada's new move—a kickflip.

Cassie: Wow, look at her fly! She could be a professional skateboarder!

Narrator: Michael and Cassie never did get the hang of skateboarding, but they did have a lot of fun on their trip to the city. When it was over, they invited Jada, Aaron, and Olivia to come to *their* home sometime. A few months later, the city cousins paid their country cousins a visit.

Olivia: Hi, Michael and Cassie! What a wonderful place to live, with all the trees, open fields, and fresh air! And you can make all the noise you want, because you don't have to worry about disturbing the neighbors.

Jada: What are we going to do for fun out here, watch grass grow?

Michael: Cassie and I planned plenty of fun, country style. For starters, let's head down to the barn and ride horses.

Olivia: But I don't know how to ride a horse!

Aaron: It can't be that hard. All you do is sit on the saddle, grab those leather things, and say, "Giddyup."

Narrator: Down at the barn, the kids looked at the horses in their stalls.

Michael: Which horse do you want to ride? This one is named Lightning Bolt, that one is Tornado, and the one kicking and snorting in the corner stall is Avalanche.

Aaron: I don't want to ride any of them! Those horses are gigantic. They could squash me like a bug if they wanted!

Olivia: And they look mean—see how they toss their heads and roll their eyes?

Cassie: They aren't mean, just high-spirited. Here, Aaron, take this sugar cube and feed it to Lightning Bolt. Just make sure you hold your hand flat so he doesn't nip you accidentally.

Aaron: No way! Look at his huge teeth! He could bite my arm off!

Olivia: Cassie, horses don't eat people, right? Aren't horses vegetarians?

Michael: Jada, which horse do you want to ride? Or are you afraid, too?

Jada: I'm not afraid of any old horse. It's just that . . . I hurt my hand back at the house. Yeah, that's right—I twisted my wrist when I was opening the door. So I don't think I can hold those leather things to drive the horse.

Michael: Those are *reins*, and you don't *drive* a horse, you *ride* it.

Jada: Whatever. I'm injured, so I guess I'd better stay right here on the ground.

Olivia: Cassie, what are those three little horses over there? Babies?

Cassie: No, those are our old ponies: Marshmallow, Dandelion, and Lumpy. They're not much fun anymore. They're old and slow, and you can't get them to run.

Olivia: (*quickly*) I'll take Marshmallow.

Aaron: (*quickly*) I'll take Dandelion.

Jada: (*quickly*) I'll take Lumpy.

Michael: Jada, I thought your wrist was twisted.

Jada: It will probably be okay on Lumpy. Those other horses might bump my injured hand, but Lumpy looks safe—I mean, he looks all right.

Narrator: The five cousins started on their ride, walking slowly because of the ponies. Michael and Cassie led the way into the woods.

Aaron: Wow, is *that* your tree house? It's about a million miles high!

11

Olivia: I don't see how you're supposed to get up there without an elevator. You don't have to climb those wobbly-looking boards nailed to the tree, do you?

Michael: Those boards aren't wobbly; my dad and I fastened them tight, with long wood screws. They're perfectly safe—but if you want, you can climb the rope instead.

Aaron: I'm not climbing that old rope! What if I slip?

Cassie: What about you, Olivia? Want to climb up? There's not much time to play because it's getting late, but you can try it out for a minute.

Olivia: No, thanks—I think I'll stay right here on good old Marshmallow.

Jada: That tree house isn't any higher than the big half pipe at the skate park! I'm not afraid. Step aside and let me up that ladder!

Narrator: Jada dismounted and walked over to the tree. She climbed slowly up the ladder, careful never to look down. At the top, she crawled through the hole in the floor and stood up. Finally, she was in the tree house.

Cassie: Jada, how's the view up there?

Jada: (*shakily*) Fine.

Michael: You should probably come on down; it's getting dark and we need to get back home. We can come back to the tree house tomorrow.

Jada: Um . . . I can't get down! It's too high!

Cassie: But you climbed up without any problem!

Jada: That was different. Now I can see how far it is to the ground.

Michael: You went higher than that when you were on the half pipe at the skate park.

Jada: But I can't skate off this thing, and there aren't any stairs to walk down. The only way off is that flimsy rope or those rickety boards.

Michael: I told you that the boards aren't rickety!

Olivia: It sure does get dark fast out here in the country. What was that awful honking noise?

Cassie: A heron, down by the creek.

Aaron: What's a heron—some kind of bear?

Cassie: No, it's a large water bird with long legs.

Jada: (*panicking*) That didn't sound like any bird to me! I want out of here! Somebody call the fire department!

Michael: Jada, stay calm. Cassie and I will help you.

Jada: Cassie, what are you doing? Don't come up here with me, or you might accidentally knock me off!

Cassie: I'm going to hold you so you won't fall. Now, lie down on your stomach and slide your legs through the hole.

Jada: I can't! I won't be able to see where I'm going!

Michael: I'm right here on the ladder below you, Jada. I'll help place your feet on the rungs.

Jada: All right, I'm lying down—oh no, do you hear the boards creaking? The floor's going to break!

Cassie: No, it's not—you're doing fine, Jada.

Narrator: Michael and Cassie helped their cousin climb down safely.

Jada: Whew! It feels so good to be on solid ground. Cassie, Michael—I was wrong about you. You're not scaredy-cats at all. I can't believe you two ride those wild horses and climb up and down this tree all the time.

Cassie: I guess it's like what Aaron said about the subway. If you live here, you get used to it.

Jada: Anyway, I'm sorry I was disrespectful. Life out here can be a lot more exciting than I thought. Next time I meet people who are different than me, I won't be so quick to judge them.

Narrator: The five cousins rode their horses and ponies back to the barn.

Michael: Jada, you don't have to worry about being bored here because Cassie and I have lots of plans. Tomorrow we can go rock climbing, or my dad can take us canoeing.

Jada: Not me! I have a big day planned. Lumpy and I are going to relax and sit around and watch the grass grow!

The End